降击神通

AVATAR

THE LAST AIRBENDER.

THE LOST SCROLLS: EARTH

BY MICHAEL TEITELBAUM
ILLUSTRATED BY SHANE L. JOHNSON
BASED ON SCREENPLAYS BY
MATT HUBBARD AND JOHN O'BRYAN

SIMON SPOTLIGHT/NICKELODEON
NEW YORK   LONDON   TORONTO   SYDNEY

Based on the TV series *Nickelodeon Avatar: The Last Airbender*™ as seen on Nickelodeon®

SIMON SPOTLIGHT
An imprint of Simon & Schuster Children's Publishing Division
1230 Avenue of the Americas, New York, New York 10020

Manufactured in the United States of America
First Edition 10 9 8 7 6 5 4 3 2 1
ISBN-13: 978-1-4169-1877-6
ISBN-10: 1-4169-1877-9
Library of Congress Catalog Card Number 2006925119

Prologue

降击神通

IF YOU ARE READING THIS,
you have uncovered one of the four hidden scrolls
I have compiled about the world of Avatar. This
scroll contains sacred stories, legends, and facts
that I have gathered so far about the proud nation
of the Earth Kingdom—its history, its culture, and the
great tales of its past and present. I hope that this
information will be as useful and intriguing to you as
it is to me. As a great friend of the Earth Kingdom,
I ask that you keep this scroll safe, and share it only
with those you trust. Beware, for there are many
who wish to expose its secrets. . . .

Introduction

降
击
神
通

Long ago there was balance between the four nations of the world—the Water Tribes, the Earth Kingdom, the Fire Nation, and the Air Nomads. Within these nations, there are people who have the ability to manipulate their culture's native element. They call themselves Waterbenders, Earthbenders, Firebenders, and Airbenders. But only the Avatar can bend all four elements. When the Avatar dies, his or her spirit is reborn into a bender of the next nation, following the cycle of Water, Earth, Fire, and Air. This cycle provides a natural balance and keeps any one nation from growing more powerful than another.

The four nations lived together in harmony until the most recent Avatar, Avatar Roku, died. Seizing the opportunity before the next Avatar, an Airbender, could be found and trained, the Fire

Nation—led by Fire Lord Sozin—launched a global war designed to eliminate the other three nations. Harnessing the energy of a passing comet to give him incredible power, Sozin attacked the Water, Air, and Earth nations at the same time.

Only the Avatar had the skill to stop the ruthless Fire Nation. But when the world needed him most, he disappeared. The war raged on for a hundred years, and hope began to fade from the world. . . .

And then the Avatar returned. The Avatar's spirit was reborn into a twelve-year-old Airbender named Aang, who had been frozen in an iceberg for a hundred years. The new Avatar was discovered by a young Waterbender from the South Pole, Katara, and her brother, Sokka. Now, together, they journey around the world to help Aang complete his Avatar training so he can save the world from the Fire Nation.

I first heard this legend while visiting the Southern Water Tribe. It recounts how a courageous young Waterbender, Katara, empowered an oppressed group of Earthbenders to stand up to the Fire Nation.

Revolt of the Earthbenders
LEGEND 1

My name is Katara. I'm a Waterbender from the Southern Water Tribe. My brother Sokka and I are journeying with Aang, the Avatar. We always wind up experiencing some pretty amazing and sometimes frightening things. But this story is by far my favorite because it's all about the power of courage.

We were on our way to the North Pole in search of a Waterbending master. One day at our campsite, we heard a loud booming sound nearby and decided to find out what it was. In a clearing, we saw a teenage boy lifting rocks and then slamming them to bits on the ground without touching them. He was Earthbending!

I had never seen a real Earthbender use his skills. I got the same thrill I always get watching a true bender at work. But when I yelled a friendly hello, he turned and ran away!

We followed the road the boy had gone down and soon came to a village. We were getting supplies in the village store when the boy came in.

"Where have you been, Haru?" the woman behind the counter asked. "You're late. Get started on your chores."

The boy seemed shocked and disappointed to see us again. When we asked him about his Earthbending,

both he and his mother froze. Haru's mother turned to him, looking very upset.

"You know how dangerous that is!" Haru's mother said. "You know what would happen if they caught you Earthbending!"

I was trying to figure out who this "they" she mentioned was and what was wrong with someone Earthbending in an Earth Kingdom village when I was startled by a loud banging on the front door. Then three Fire Nation soldiers bullied their way in and demanded money from Haru's mother. She said that she had already paid them for the week, but they began threatening to burn the place down. Defeated, she gave them what few coins she had left and they exited the store.

I was outraged.

"They're thugs!" Haru cried out. "They steal from us. And everyone here is too much of a coward to do anything about it!"

"Quiet, Haru," she said. "Don't talk like that."

I pointed out that Haru was an Earthbender. He could certainly help, even organize an uprising of Earthbenders to chase the Fire Nation from their village, but she just looked at me and said that Earthbending was forbidden, and that Haru must never do it again.

I was stunned. I thought about what it would be like if I wasn't allowed to Waterbend—it would be like asking someone to stop breathing or thinking. Bending is a part of who we are.

So I asked her what the Fire Nation soldiers would do to them for Earthbending that they hadn't already done.

"They could take Haru away," she answered, "like they took away his father."

I was shocked. The Fire Nation had taken his father and imprisoned him. I knew exactly how it felt to lose a parent, as I had lost my own mother. And my father had left to fight in the war. I felt my anger growing. There had to be something I could do!

After that, Haru showed us where we could spend the night, but said we would have to leave immediately when the sun came up. Haru and I went for a walk and shared our thoughts.

"I'm sorry. I didn't know about your father," I explained.

"It's funny," he said. "The way you were talking back in the store reminded me of my father. He was very courageous."

I was flattered that Haru would compare me to the man he admired so much. Did he sense a courage within me, too?

"When the Fire Nation attacked, my father and the other Earthbenders were outnumbered ten to one, but they fought back anyway. After the attack, they rounded up my father and every other Earthbender and took them away," Haru said. "We haven't seen them since."

I told Haru that his father sounded like a great man. He smiled, but seemed to grow even sadder. He told me the only way he feels close to his father is when he's Earthbending, because his father taught him everything he knows. Then I understood why Haru had to Earthbend even though it was forbidden. I told him about my mother and showed him the necklace that my mom gave me. I told him that it was all I had left of her.

"It's beautiful," he said. "But it's not enough, is it?"

I shook my head and stared down at the necklace, longing to see her again. "No, it's not."

Then, out of nowhere, came a cry for help. We dashed toward the sound, down to a mine, where we discovered an old man buried under a pile of rocks. We tried to pull the man free but couldn't. I looked around and saw no one. Then I pleaded with Haru to use his Earthbending skills to help the old man. After some reluctance, he finally agreed, and with a swift and powerful Earthbending move, he pushed the rocks back into the mine, freeing the man.

We went back to the village and said good night. We needed a good night's sleep for our journey the following day. The next morning, Haru's mother told us that Fire Nation troops came and dragged Haru away in the middle of the night. We were horrified!

The old man Haru had saved had turned him in for Earthbending.

It was all my fault! I had forced him to Earthbend. I was the reason he became a prisoner of the Fire Nation! Well, I was not about to accept that—I was going to rescue him! The only way to do that was to get captured by the Fire Nation and become a prisoner myself.

I came up with a plan to make it look like I was Earthbending—and it worked! With a little help from Aang and Sokka, the Fire Nation troops thought they caught me in mid-Earthbending move and hauled me away.

But at that moment I was scared. Where were they taking me, and how would I ever get out? What made me think I could do this on my own?

The Fire Nation troops shipped me to a metal prison rig out in the middle of the ocean. There were hundreds of imprisoned Earthbenders being held captive, forced to build ships for the Fire Nation, unable to use their bending abilities. It was a dreary and depressing place, and the second I arrived I remembered what had brought me there. I had to let go of my fears and help get these people out of here.

When I found Haru he was surprised to see me. I told him I felt responsible for getting him caught, that I had come to rescue him and everyone else as well.

At dinner that evening, Haru took me to meet his father, Tyro. When I asked Tyro what his escape plan was, he looked at me like I was crazy, and said his plan was to wait out the war until they could go home. It seemed like Tyro and the others had already given up. I knew that the Earthbenders were a proud, strong people. I couldn't believe they would just lie down and accept this horrible treatment as their fate.

"I admire your courage, Katara," Tyro said. His

voice sounded tired. He spoke like a defeated man. "But people's lives are at stake here. The warden is a ruthless man and he won't stand for any rebellion. I'm sorry, but we're powerless."

I was not going to accept this. I jumped up onto a table and banged my spoon and bowl together to get everyone's attention. Then I spoke, loudly and forcefully. I told the Earthbenders that every child in my Water Tribe village was rocked to sleep with stories of the brave Earth Kingdom and the courageous Earthbenders who guarded its borders. I urged them, saying that although the Fire Nation has made them powerless, no one had the power to take away their courage. I could feel my own courage build as I spoke. I said it was the strength

of their hearts that made them who they were, and that the time to fight back was now!

I thought I was getting through to them, but when I had finished, this sea of blank faces stared up at me as if I hadn't said a word. After a moment, they turned back to their dinners and their quiet conversation.

After dinner we all returned to our quarters. But I couldn't fall asleep. What was wrong with these people? Had their spirit truly been crushed? Downhearted, I slipped into my bedroll and cried myself to sleep.

I was awakened in the middle of the night by Sokka, who had flown with Aang on his flying bison, Appa, to rescue me. But I told them that I wasn't leaving without the others. We tried to come up with some way for them to fight back, but the whole rig was made of metal. Then Sokka pointed to smoke pouring from a smokestack. "I'll bet they're burning coal here. In other words . . . Earth!"

Sometimes Sokka can be so smart! I really had to hand it to my brother. He explained that there must be a huge pile of coal in the silo and that the system that fueled the rig was ventilated. He said he'd close off all the vents but one, and told Aang to go down and Airbend the coal up to the surface. The force would cause it all to shoot out of the only open vent, giving the Earthbenders a ton of coal to fight with. Just after Aang had gone down to do his part, the horrible warden and his guards stepped up to Sokka and me. Just as their verbal threats started to turn into action, we felt a low rumbling underneath our feet. Suddenly a mountain of coal shot from the air vent. Aang had done his job.

"Here's your chance, Earthbenders!" I shouted.

"Take it! Your fate is in your own hands," I said, hoping they'd find some courage inside themselves.

The silence was broken by a sickening laugh from the warden. "Foolish girl," he cackled. "You thought a few inspirational words and some coal would change these people? Look at their blank, hopeless faces. Their spirits were broken a long time ago. You've failed!"

There was nothing more I could do. They would spend the rest of their lives there. And so would I. But at that moment I really didn't care.

Then, as the warden walked away, a lump of coal struck him in the back of the head. He spun around, furious, and saw what I saw—Haru controlling three pieces of coal floating in a circle above his hand.

I felt my spirit rushing back. I had gotten through to Haru. But would the others follow?

Enraged, the warden shot a stream of flames right at Haru. Suddenly, a huge wall of coal rose up, blocking the flame. Haru and I looked over at the same time to see that Tyro had Earthbended a wall to save his son's life.

"Show no mercy!" cried the warden as he and his guards let loose their Firebending blasts.

"For the Earth Kingdom!" Tyro shouted. "Attack!"

Inspired, the other Earthbenders joined in and blocked each fire blast with coal. Finally, the Earthbenders created one huge disc of coal, scooped up the warden and his guards with it, and then hovered it over the ocean.

"No! Please! I can't swim!" cried the warden.

"Don't worry," replied Tyro. "I hear cowards float."

Then he dissolved the large disc, and the warden and his guards plunged into the churning sea.

I was so proud of Haru and the others, and so glad I could help in some small way.

"I want to thank you for saving me," Haru said as Aang, Sokka, and I prepared to leave on Appa. "For saving us."

"All it took was a little coal," I said, blushing uncontrollably.

"It wasn't the coal, Katara. It was you," Haru said.

Then Tyro stepped beside us. "Thank you for helping me find my courage, Katara of the Water Tribe," he said. "My family, and everyone here, owes you much." Then Tyro bowed to me. I couldn't believe such a wise and talented bender was bowing to me! I was so honored.

Haru asked me to come back to his village with him, but as much as I wanted to stay with him, I knew I couldn't. As Sokka, Aang, and I flew off on Appa, I realized how powerful courage is, and how much I had within myself. And for the first time in a long time I felt hopeful about the future.

This is the basic information I have gathered about the Earth Kingdom, its people, its cities, its beliefs, and its customs.

The Earth Kingdom and Its Philosophy

The people of the Earth Kingdom are proud and strong and adhere to a philosophy of peaceful coexistence and cooperation with the other nations of the world. Earthbenders use their abilities for defense and industry and have fiercely defended their cities against attacks by the Fire Nation.

EARTH KINGDOM INSIGNIA

The symbol of the Earth Kingdom is a square within a larger circle, within a still larger square, which symbolizes both the literal and figurative depth of the Earth Kingdom. It represents the many layers of deep rock and coal that Earthbenders manipulate and use to run their great cities, and the depth of their commitment to a peaceful and productive way of life.

EARTH KINGDOM CITIES

There are some great cities that spread across the huge expanse that makes up the Earth Kingdom. The Kingdom's capital, Ba Sing Se, is led by the Earth king and is the largest of all Earth Kingdom cities. The city of Omashu is led by King Bumi. The village of Kyoshi is located on an island and is home to a great tribe of female warriors, and Gaoling is a wealthy city full of commerce and culture. It is also home to Master Yu's Earthbending Academy, where Earthbending tournaments are held.

BA SING SE

GAOLING

SEASON

The Earth Nation's dominant season is spring, the time when many living things on Earth are reborn. More Earthbenders are born during spring than any other season. Earthbenders are also strongest during the spring.

NATURAL RESOURCES/FOOD

An abundance of fresh vegetables grows in the rich fertile soil, and fruit and nut trees are plentiful. Animals thrive in the lush forests and farmlands, providing beef and poultry to add to the fruits and vegetables. Rock and stone are two of the Earth Kingdom's greatest natural resources, and are Earthbended into everything from tools to entire cities. Coal is mined in certain Earth Kingdom villages, providing fuel. Their forests are also used for fuel and for building.

INDUSTRIES

Architecture, farming, carpentry, hunting, and coal mining are important Earth Kingdom industries. The Earth people have developed an advanced trade and commerce system, as well as sophisticated sewage and mail delivery systems in Omashu.

ANIMALS

The Earth Kingdom is home to a wide variety of animals including cats, moles, voles, gophers, hoppy-possums (a cross between frogs and possums), hippos, flying boars, creeping slime (an algaelike mass that crawls up the walls of the sewers in Omashu), monstrous canyon crawlers that live in the Great Divide, and insects such as ants, leech-a-pillars, and butterflies.

HOPPY-POSSUM

BUTTERFLY

LEECH-A-PILLAR

CANYON CRAWLERS

LOCATION

The Earth Kingdom is by far the largest of all four nations.

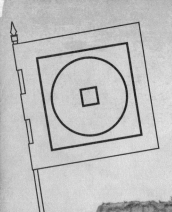

The Art of Earthbending

Earthbenders use the Earth as their weapon. Extremely muscular, they use their own physical strength to power their attacks. The source of their power is the Earth itself—the very rock that makes up their planet combines with their own physical abilities to give an Earthbender his or her great power.

ANCIENT MARTIAL ARTS INFLUENCE

Earthbending uses techniques taken from the Hung Gar style of kung fu. Like this ancient martial arts discipline, Earthbending is known for its strong stances rooted in the ground. Hung Gar kung fu is based on the movements of animals, including the tiger, which Earthbenders use when initiating hard blows, and the crane, which Earthbenders use to land gently back on the Earth.

EARTHBENDING TECHNIQUES

Earthbenders use many techniques during combat or construction.

They can strike the ground with their hands or feet, causing small tremors or earthquakes.

They can stomp the ground hard, causing a boulder to form and spring up, which they then kick toward an opponent.

They can also bend the Earth in order to catapult themselves into the air, and then soften the Earth to cushion their landings. They can open cracks in the ground to swallow up an opponent, raise slabs of stone from the Earth to use as defensive walls (these are especially good at blocking fire), and levitate stones to propel them at opponents.

Earthbenders can also magnetize their limbs to stone, allowing them to climb sheer walls or cliffs.

An Earthbender has eighty-five jings, or choices of how to direct his or her energy. Of these, the neutral jing—listening and waiting for the right moment to strike—is the most important. The highest-level Earthbenders can change solid ground into quicksand to entrap approaching enemies.

WEAKNESS

Earthbenders' most significant weakness is their inability to manipulate metal. The Fire Nation has exploited this weakness by attempting to surround Earthbenders with metal armor, ships, and forts.

GROUP EARTHBENDING MOVES

Earthbenders can combine their power using group movements to create a massive wall or huge boulder from many small pieces of coal, which can then be propelled toward an entire squadron of enemy troops. One Earthbender can lift a steady stream of small pieces of coal into the air, while another shoots the rocks forward at an enemy. They can also manipulate the coal into a large, flat disc, which can scoop up and carry away enemies.

This is a tale of the Avatar's arrival in the great Earth Kingdom city of Omashu. Passed down by the Avatar himself, the story tells us of the valuable lesson he learned, one that would aid him in all of his future travels.

The Kingdom of Omashu
LEGEND 2

I'm Aang, the Avatar. When I was younger, I used to come to the Earth Kingdom city of Omashu to visit my friend Bumi. I returned to Omashu for the first time in one hundred years with my good friends Katara and Sokka on our way to the North Pole, and boy, what a crazy visit it was!

My heart soared as I stood on a hilltop looking down at Omashu, towering over the valley below. The city was carved out of a mountain, and a long, stone bridge wound its way from the valley up to the city's massive front gate. I ran up to the gate ready to enter, but as always, Katara was worried about me and what would happen if people found out I was the Avatar. So I put on a disguise: a mustache and wig made from Appa's hair! It was so itchy, it drove me nuts. I don't know how Appa stands it!

But it worked. The guards used their awesome Earthbending powers to open the huge stone gates of Omashu and we were inside the city!

The city was covered by a vast delivery system of stone chutes for mail, packages, and anything else they needed to move from the highest parts of the city to the lowest. Earthbending brought the carts up and gravity brought them down.

"So they get their mail on time," Sokka said, uninterested.

"They *do* get their mail on time," I replied. "But my friend Bumi found an even better use for these chutes." One hundred years ago, Bumi had introduced me to a world of possibilities.

"Instead of seeing what others want you to see," Bumi had said, "try opening your mind to the possibilities. It's not just a mail chute; it's the world's greatest superslide!"

"Bumi, you're a mad genius!" I'd cried. We climbed

into a delivery cart and zoomed down the chutes, racing our way to the bottom. We had a blast!

So I talked Katara and Sokka into taking just one ride with me. Katara gripped the cart for dear life, but I was having a ball. I had it all under control until my Airbending lifted our cart completely out of the chute! We sailed through the air, crashed through a potter's house (I felt really bad about that), and then crashed into a cabbage vendor (I felt bad about that, too). We finally came to a stop, only to be met by the king's guards. They took us before the king for our punishment.

The king was a really old man. He looked weak and fragile, and I wondered how he had come to rule over such a powerful kingdom. I thought for sure we'd end up in jail, and it would all be my fault, but then the king announced his judgment.

"Throw them a feast!" he proclaimed.

And they did! The king kept eyeing me suspiciously at the table, and then he hurled a huge chicken leg right at me! I didn't have time to think. I just caught

the chicken leg in a ball of air, stopping it from pelting me in the face. Suddenly I realized I had made a big mistake. I had put us in danger.

"It appears we have an Airbender in our presence," the king announced. "And not just any Airbender—the Avatar!"

I admitted to the king that I was the Avatar and started backing away toward the door. Katara and Sokka followed me, but the guards blocked our way. It was no use.

"Tomorrow the Avatar will face three deadly challenges," the king announced. "But now the guards will show you to your chambers."

I awoke the next morning and Katara and Sokka were gone. I demanded to know where they were.

"The king will free them if you complete the challenges," the guard said.

"And if I fail?" I asked, fearing the answer.

"He didn't say."

My friends' safety depended on my ability to overcome whatever challenges the king had planned. I couldn't fail. This was one of those times I wished that someone else was the Avatar.

The guard led me into a large stone room, where Katara and Sokka were being held by two guards. Their fate rested in my hands.

Then the king asked me what I thought of his

outfit. I didn't know what to say, but I wasn't about to tell him that I thought it was ugly. In the end, I settled on fine. He smiled and told me I passed my first test. I was so relieved! But he was just toying with me—he said I'd passed the test, not the challenge. He seemed to enjoy watching me suffer. I was so furious that I unleashed a powerful Airbending move and demanded he give me back my friends now.

"I thought you might refuse, so I gave your friends some special souvenirs," the king said as the guards slid crystal rings on Katara and Sokka.

"Those rings are made of pure Jennamite," the king explained. "They are also known as creeping crystals. These crystals grow remarkably fast. By nightfall your friends will be completely encased in crystal. I can stop it, but only if you cooperate."

I had no choice. My recklessness got us into this mess, and now my skills would have to get us out of it. I told the king that I'd do whatever he wanted.

He led me into a huge cavern. Sharp stalagmites

jutted up from the cave floor, and equally sharp stalactites hung down from the ceiling. In the center of the cave, right in the middle of a raging waterfall, a key hung on a chain from the ceiling. A ladder rose up just below it.

"It seems I've lost my lunch box key and I'm hungry," the king said, looking right at me. "Would you mind fetching it for me?"

It didn't look too tough. I launched myself off a stalagmite and used my Airbending to speed to the base of the ladder. But the moment I entered the waterfall, I felt its raging torrent press down on me and I couldn't outmuscle it. I lost my grip and was flung out of the waterfall. It took a last-second bit of Airbending to catch myself before I fell on a sharp stalagmite.

"Oh, climbing the ladder," the king mocked me. "No one's thought of that before!"

I hated being made fun of, especially by some crazy guy who held the fate of my friends in his hands. Obviously force wasn't going to get the job done. There had to be another way. I glanced down at the stalagmite I was clutching and I got an idea. I grabbed the point, yanked hard, and the top snapped off. I hurled it toward the waterfall, following up with a powerful Airbending burst that directed the pointy rock right through the key's chain. The rock cut the chain in half and continued to soar through the air, landing in the wall above the king's head. There was the key, dangling right in front of his face!

"Here, enjoy your lunch," I said as the king took the key. "I want my friends back. Now!" I looked over and saw that the crystal was growing quickly.

"Not yet," the king replied. "I need your help with another matter. I lost my pet, Flopsie."

The king led me into another chamber, where I spotted a small, sweet-looking furry creature, which I assumed was Flopsie.

After a few minutes of chasing the little fur ball, this other huge creature came towering over me, growling and revealing long, sharp fangs and long, floppy ears. Suddenly, it started licking my face. That's when I discovered the little ball of fur wasn't Flopsie—the big, scary ball of fur was! Yikes! Good thing Flopsie turned out to be a lovable ball of fur after I stopped acting scared.

"Okay, I found your Flopsie!" I told the king.

"Guys, are you okay?" I called over to them.

"Other than the crystal slowly encasing my entire body, you mean?" Katara said, forcing a pained smile. "Doing great!"

The crystals just kept spreading. Time was running out.

"Come on!" I shouted. "I'm ready for the next challenge."

"Your final test is a duel," the king said. "And you may choose your opponent."

Suddenly two of the scariest-looking guys I'd ever seen stepped into the room. One guy carried a sharp spear, the other, an enormous ax. I didn't have much of a choice. Then I came up with a brilliant plan—at least, I thought so at the time. I pointed at the king. He was old and weak and I figured I'd be able to knock him over with a single Airbending blast.

Boy was I wrong!

The king threw off his robe, and underneath, his body was solid muscle. His Earthbending power was beyond anything I'd ever seen. He jumped into the air, and when his feet struck the ground, he sent a wave of rock rippling under me, which knocked me

halfway across the room!

The king continued his powerful attacks, sending small rocks and large boulders sailing at me. I deflected them using Airbending, but I wasn't sure how long I could keep it up!

"Typical Airbender tactic," the king taunted me. "Avoid and evade. I'd hoped the Avatar would be less predictable. Sooner or later you'll have to strike back!"

Angered by his taunts, I charged right at the king, but he forced a thick wall to spring from the ground, blocking my way. No matter which way I turned, a wall rose up to stop me. At one point he even turned the ground I was running on into quicksand! How do I get myself into these messes?

I began to run around in a tight circle repeatedly to create a spinning vortex so I could catch his rocks in it and deflect them back at him. My vortex worked, but the king just Earthbended the boulders into tiny grains of sand!

He then tore off a huge chunk of the room and flung it toward me, but my air vortex spun that right back at him too. While the king was busy disintegrating the large chunk of rock, I was able to sneak up on him and slam him with an Airbending blast that knocked him to the ground.

"Well done, Avatar," the king said. "You fight with much fire in your heart."

Then he opened a crack in the ground and fell through it. He reappeared right next to Katara and Sokka, who were now, aside from their faces, completely covered in crystal. I had done it. I had finished the challenges in time.

"You passed all my tests," he said. "Answer this one question and I'll set your friends free," the king said. I was furious! I had already passed all of his tests! He kept changing the rules, and I wasn't about to take it. But no matter how much I protested, he just smirked and said, "What's the point of tests if you don't learn anything?

"What is my name?" the king asked.

How should I know? Talk about an unfair challenge!

"Think about the challenges," Katara suggested as the crystal started closing in on her face. "What did you learn? Maybe it's some kind of riddle."

"Well, they weren't straightforward," I said. "To solve each test I had to think differently from how I would normally."

I thought about the king for a moment, and then it struck me like a thunderbolt. "I know his name!" I announced. I was sure I was right.

I turned toward the king. "As you said a long time ago, I had to open my mind to the possibilities. Bumi, you're a mad genius!"

Imagine that! My old friend Bumi, the king of Omashu!

I was so happy. I thought I'd never see him again!

"It's good to see you again, Aang. You haven't changed a bit . . . literally," he said, smiling.

"Uh, a little help over here!" Katara yelled, just as the crystal enclosed her face.

With a tiny wave of his hand, Bumi shattered the crystal surrounding Katara and Sokka. Then he picked up a piece and popped it into his mouth. "Jennamite is made of rock candy," he said. "Delicious."

"Why did you do all this instead of just telling Aang who you were?" Sokka asked.

Bumi said that as the Avatar, I have a pretty huge task ahead of me, and that he hoped that his little tests would help me meet those challenges by thinking like a mad genius. Maybe he's right!

Before we left Omashu, Bumi and I took a long-overdue ride in a cart down one of the mail chutes. As I sped along the chute, I thought that when the time came for me to learn Earthbending, I couldn't find a better teacher than my old pal Bumi!

The Legend of the First Earthbenders

HOW OMASHU CAME TO BE

42

The legend of the first Earthbenders, also known as the "Legend of the Two Lovers," is as old as Earthbending itself. Two lovers from warring villages were separated by a mountain and forbidden to see each other. These lovers learned Earthbending from the first Earthbenders, the badger-moles who lived in the mountain, and thus became the first human Earthbenders. They used their newfound abilities to carve an elaborate system of tunnels through the mountain so they could be together. When the man was killed in the war, the woman became so furious that she unleashed a display of Earthbending that could have destroyed both villages. Eventually, she used her powers to end the war and both villages helped her build a new city out of the mountain where they could all live in peace. The woman's name was Oma. The man's name was Shu, and so the city was called Omashu.

THE GATES OF OMASHU

Omashu's massive stone gates can only be opened by skilled Earthbenders. There are three gates, one behind the other, that stand at the entrance to the city. Each gate is five feet thick and towers over thirty feet into the air. Working in tandem, the two guards use Earthbending to separate the two halves of the first gate.

KYOSHI

The Earth Kingdom village of Kyoshi, named for the Avatar who was born there four hundred years before, is located on an island in the South Sea. The island is primarily a fishing port and is visited by many travelers and traders. Its remote location and small population have kept it safe from Fire Nation attacks. The village has a team of female Kyoshi warriors, who stand ready to serve and protect the people of the island.

KYOSHI WARRIORS

Avatar Kyoshi, a powerful Earthbending woman, taught the fighting and defensive techniques now used by the Kyoshi warriors who defend the island. In her honor, the village has a huge statue of her. Because of her great influence, all the warriors on Kyoshi are female. Their fighting style is about turning the enemy's force against himself, not about overpowering their opponent. Their weapon is the fan and their traditional outfits and painted faces, modeled after Kabuki theater, are designed to intimidate their opponents.

The following legend was found in the journal kept by the Avatar and his friends about their travels. One memorable adventure through the Earth Kingdom taught everyone a valuable lesson about how important it is to stand behind your people in times of danger.

The Great Divide
LEGEND 3

46

My buddy Aang is a pretty smart guy. Of course, he's also the Avatar, so that's no surprise. One of the smartest things I ever saw him do was make peace between two feuding Earth tribes, the Gan Jins and the Zhangs. By the way, I'm Sokka, just in case there's any confusion about who's writing this. I'm a warrior from the Southern Water Tribe and I'm traveling with Aang, the Avatar, and my sister, Katara, on our way to find them a Waterbending master.

We just finished crossing the Great Divide, this huge canyon of rocks, with the feuding Earth tribes. Boy, an experience like that really reminds me how important it is for us to fight together against our common enemy—the Fire Nation—and not get sidetracked by silly arguments, no matter how frustrating some know-it-alls can be!

Take my sister, for example. She's a Waterbender. And she can be quite a pain sometimes! Just last night, I was setting up the tent in our campsite when she basically demanded I put the tarp on top of the tent. As if I needed her instructions! She has this idea in her head that she knows everything. I tried to tell her it was the dry season and we wouldn't need it, but she got mad and then we got into a huge fight.

That's when Aang came back from gathering dinner. When he realized we were fighting, he actually gave some pretty good advice. He said that harsh words wouldn't solve problems. Only action could. Then he suggested that we switch jobs. We both agreed. I knew I could gather more firewood than she could any day. And I couldn't wait to see her try to put up the tent!

"You see that," Aang said. "Settling feuds and making peace. All in a day's work for the Avatar."

Little did Aang know, he'd soon have a much bigger feud to settle.

The next day we came to the Great Divide, the biggest canyon in the world. Katara was all impressed. Me, I found the whole thing boring. I mean it's just a bunch of rocks! I just wanted to get across the thing, and flying over on Appa was the fastest way to do it.

But then this guy came running up to us; he seemed annoyed.

"If you're looking for the canyon guide, I was here first," the guy said. "He's an Earthbender and the only way across the canyon is with his help. And he's taking my tribe across the canyon next."

"All right, calm down," I said. Jeez!

"You wouldn't be calm if the Fire Nation destroyed your home and forced you to flee," he said. "My whole tribe has to walk a thousand miles to the Earth capital city of Ba Sing Se."

Then Katara spotted a tribe coming toward us.

"Is that your tribe?" she asked.

"It most certainly is not!" he replied. He sounded really annoyed. "I'm a scout for the Gan Jin tribe. That wretched-looking group is the Zhang tribe, a bunch of lowlife thieves. They've been the enemies of my tribe for a hundred years."

When the Zhang tribe arrived, they started arguing with this guy about who should go across the canyon first.

"Where are the rest of the Gan Jin tribe?" the Zhang leader asked. "Still tidying up their campsite?"

These guys really didn't like each other. But I didn't see why this was our problem. We had Appa. Then the canyon guide showed up, followed by the rest of the Gan Jins, and a big argument broke out over who should cross the canyon first.

"We should go first," the Zhang leader said. "We have sick people that need shelter."

"We have old people who are weary from traveling," the Gan Jin scout argued. So Aang stepped up to do his Avatar peacemaking routine. His suggestion that the two tribes share the guide and travel across together went over like a Fire Nation ship in a Water Tribe village.

"We'd rather be taken by the Fire Nation than travel with those stinking thieves," said the Gan Jin leader.

"We wouldn't travel with you tyrants anyway!" said the Zhang leader.

Finally Aang got mad. "All right, here's the deal!" he yelled. "You're all going down together, and Appa, my flying bison, will fly all the sick and the elderly from both tribes across the canyon. Does that seem fair?"

At first I was impressed by Aang's skill. But then I realized what this meant for me—I was going to have to walk across the enormous canyon on foot! And then came even more bad news. The guide told us that no one could bring any food down into the canyon because it would attract dangerous predators. Sounded like this was going to be some fun trip!

We descended into the canyon, following a narrow

winding ledge that ran along the sheer rock face. When we came to a huge gap in the pathway, the guide used his Earthbending powers to extend large chunks of rock from the canyon wall to complete the missing pieces of the path. Later, when a rockslide almost buried us, the guide Earthbended the avalanche of stones completely away from us. Talk about a handy guy to have around when you're crossing a rock-filled canyon! No wonder the tribes didn't want to cross it without him. Finally, we reached the bottom of the canyon wall safely. Suddenly a giant monster that looked like a cross between a spider and a crocodile crawled down the canyon wall and snatched the guide in its jaws.

I immediately grabbed my boomerang and flung it at the beast. After all, I am a warrior, and someone had to protect our guide. My weapon struck the creature right in the eye, forcing it to drop the Earthbender. It was an amazing shot! But before I could rejoice in my skill, the creature turned and charged at me!

Katara swatted the beast with a Waterbending move, but it didn't work. The creature turned its big ugly mouth toward her and snapped. Nobody attacks my sister, no matter how big of a pain she is! As I reached back for my boomerang again,

Aang leaped in, blowing the creature away with an Airbending blast, causing it to cower back inside a distant cave.

"What was that?" Aang asked as we all hurried over to the guide.

"Canyon crawler," the guide gasped, obviously in pain. "And there's sure to be more."

Both of the guide's arms were broken, and without his arms, he couldn't Earthbend—which meant we were trapped in the canyon. I knew coming down here on foot was a bad idea! I was really mad. I thought the whole point of not bringing any food down here was so that we wouldn't have to deal with creatures like that. If I had known other people were bringing food down here, I sure would have brought a snack. The question was, who was the culprit?

"It's the Zhangs!" cried the Gan Jin leader. "They brought food with them!"

"What!" cried the Zhang leader. "If there's anyone who can't go without food for a day it's you pampered Gan Jins!"

That's when the two tribes started arguing again, each one saying that they wouldn't take one more step with the other. I thought that Katara and I fought a lot, but these guys were ridiculous.

"Stop!" Aang finally yelled to be heard over all the shouting. "I thought I could help you all get along, but I see now that that is impossible! We'll have to split up. Gan Jins, you travel on one side of the canyon, Zhangs on the other."

Then Aang asked me to travel with the Zhangs and Katara to travel with the Gan Jins so we could try to find out why they hated each other so much. That was fine with me, as long as we just kept moving.

That night, I watched the Zhangs set up their campsite. None of them put tarps on the tents. They said they didn't need to because it was the dry season. And they told me that they like to use the tarps as blankets. Finally, someone who understood me! I really liked these guys. And I couldn't wait to tell Katara that she was totally wrong about the whole tarp thing.

Then, I liked these Zhangs even more when one of them pulled out food and offered some to me! Man, was it delicious. The Zhang leader told me that the Gan Jins thought so poorly of the Zhangs that the Gan Jins probably brought food along because they assumed the Zhangs would—which is why the Zhangs brought their food.

Whatever, all I know is I was hungry and that roasted leg of something or other was really good! Anyway, as I munched, the Zhang leader told me why the Zhangs hated the Gan Jins so much.

One hundred years ago, a Zhang named Wei Jin was traveling when he saw that a member of the Gan Jins named Jin Wei had collapsed just outside the village. Jin Wei was carrying an orb, sacred to his people, back to their village. Wei Jin stopped to help Jin Wei, who told Wei Jin to bring the orb to the Gan Jin village. Wei Jin promised to send help back for the injured Jin Wei. But as soon as Wei Jin crossed the border into Gan Jin territory, instead of thanking him for delivering their sacred orb, the Gan Jins threw him into jail for twenty years! The Zhangs never forgave the Gan Jins for this great injustice.

No wonder the Zhangs hated those Gan Jins. What an awful thing to do. I'd be pretty mad too if they

did that to one of my fellow Water Tribe warriors. Besides, they gave me food, so how bad could they be?

The next morning the Zhangs and the Gan Jins met near a tall rock.

"Sokka, Katara, will these people cooperate long enough to get out of the canyon?" Aang asked us.

"I don't think so, Aang," Katara said. "The Zhangs really wronged the Gan Jins. Long ago, a Zhang named Wei Jin ambushed and attacked a Gan Jin named Jin Wei just to steal the Gan Jins' sacred orb."

I was shocked. How could Katara believe such an obvious lie! I tried to explain that Wei Jin was just trying to return the sacred orb to the Gan Jins but as usual, my sister wouldn't listen to me. She had made up her stubborn mind and that was that.

And we weren't the only ones arguing. The Zhangs and Gan Jins began shouting at each other again. Then they drew their weapons and began fighting. Suddenly Aang broke up the fighting with a huge Airbending move that flung the two leaders back to their sides of the canyon and forced the food they had smuggled in to fall to the ground. Aang was furious about the food, but he didn't have much time to yell before a whole bunch of canyon crawlers showed up!

Katara took my hand. "Sokka," she said, "I don't care about this stupid feud. I just want us to get out of here alive!"

"Me too. I only took their side 'cause they fed me," I admitted.

There were times when I was really glad that Katara was my sister. I knew deep down she cared more about me than about being right. I half expected a comment from her about me thinking with my stomach and not my head, but she didn't say a word. We just ran for it.

We battled the canyon crawlers the best we could, but it seemed hopeless. There was no way we could beat them—but Aang came up with a plan so we didn't have to.

Aang jumped onto a crawler's back, then guided it over to where the food had fallen. He scooped up the food and wrapped it in a sack, which he tied to a stick. Then he dangled the food in front of a crawler. When it stuck its head out to grab the food, Aang covered its mouth with one of the empty sacks that the food was in. Everyone else did the same thing. Then we pointed our sticks up the canyon wall. The crawlers chased the food right up the wall, carrying all of us on their backs!

I have to admit I was pretty creeped out riding on the back of that thing, but as long as I dangled food in front of its nose it didn't seem to be interested in me at all.

When we reached the top, Aang shouted for everyone to jump off and toss their food over the cliff, back down into the canyon, where the crawlers followed it.

"I never thought that a Gan Jin could get his hands dirty like that," the Zhang leader remarked.

"And I never thought you Zhangs were so reliable in a pinch," the Gan Jin leader said.

"Perhaps we're not so different after all," the Zhang leader commented.

"Too bad we can't rewrite history," the Gan Jin leader said. "You thieves stole our sacred orb from Jin Wei."

"You tyrants unjustly imprisoned Wei Jin!" the Zhang leader cried, yanking his hand free and grabbing his sword.

"Wait a second," Aang said, stepping in between the two leaders. "Jin Wei, Wei Jin? I know those guys," Aang said. "I might not look it, but I'm one hundred and twelve years old. I was there one hundred years ago on the day you are talking about. There seems to be a lot of confusion about what happened. First of all, Jin Wei and Wei Jin weren't enemies, they were brothers—twins, in fact. And they were eight. And most importantly, they were just playing a game.

The sacred orb from the legend? That was the ball. And the Eastern and Western gates, those were the goal posts. Jin Wei had the ball and was running to score a goal when he fell down and fumbled it. Wei Jin picked it up and started running toward the other goal, but he stepped out of bounds. So the official put him in the penalty box for two minutes, not in jail for twenty years. Don't get me wrong, Wei Jin was kind of a slob, and Jin Wei was a little bit stuffy, but they respected each other's differences enough to share the same playing field."

"I suppose it's time we forget the past," the leader of the Zhangs declared.

"And look toward the future," the leader of the Gan Jins added with a bow.

"Then let us travel to the Earth Kingdom capital together, as one tribe!" the Zhang leader declared, as they set off toward the capital.

"That was some luck that you knew Jin Wei and Wei Jin," I said.

"You could call it luck, or you could call it lying!" Aang said. "I made the whole thing up!"

Katara and I were shocked! But I have to admit, I was really impressed with Aang. He really was a great peacemaker. Even if it took a little white lie to make the peace, it was still a great strategy. Hmm . . . I wonder if he's ever duped me and Katara into forgiving one another with a made-up story like that? No way, he could never dupe me! Anyway, from now on I'm definitely going to make a point of not fighting so much over stupid things—I mean, if we spend our energy fighting against each other, how will we have the strength to fight the real enemy?

This is all that I know about the Gan Jins, the Zhangs, and the Great Divide, the largest canyon in the world.

The Great Divide

Some people have said that the canyon is the result of millions of years of erosion, but local belief teaches that the canyon was carved into the ground by Earth spirits who were angry with local farmers for not offering them proper sacrifices. The narrow path along the sheer canyon wall offers the only way down. Fraught with carnivorous creatures and missing sections of walls, the canyon is extremely dangerous and should not be crossed without the aid of the Earthbender guide. He is the only one who knows the secrets of the canyon and can re-create missing sections of the trail to allow people to cross otherwise perilous paths.

THE GAN JINS AND THE ZHANGS

The Gan Jins have always been better educated, dressed, and mannered, as well as cleaner, than their enemy tribe. For hundreds of years, they performed a sacred ritual known as the Redemption ritual, during which their sacred orb was carried from the Great Eastern Gate to the Great Western Gate, a journey that simulated the rising and setting of the sun. It was thought that this ritual purified the Gan Jins' connection to the spirits.

THE WESTERN GATE

Ever since the disappearance of their orb at the hands of a Zhang, or so they thought, they have considered the Zhangs to be dirty, lazy, slovenly people lacking in self–respect.

THE GAN JINS

THE GAN JINS' SACRED ORB

The origins of the sacred orb are unknown. With each passing year, the story of the missing orb becomes more and more blurred. It has been discussed that the orb may not have existed at all, or that if it did, it was just a simple toy for children.

Historically, the Zhang tribe is known as a sloppy and unrefined people. Much of this is due to their wild professions as outdoorsmen and hunters. However, in modern days the Zhangs have been involved in many other industries as well. Since the feud began, the Zhangs have viewed the Gan Jins as a stuffy, overly particular, and unjust people.

What they share in common is their status as refugees after having been attacked by the Fire Nation.

THE ZHANGS

Epilogue

AS I SEAL THIS SCROLL, the Fire Nation war rages on. Aang, Katara, and Sokka finally made it to the North Pole, where Katara discovered just how powerful a Waterbender she really is. The Northern Water Tribe then survived a massive attack by the Fire Nation fleet, thanks to the Avatar and the Ocean Spirit, who teamed up to wipe out an entire Fire Nation fleet.

Prince Zuko of the Fire Nation is still considered an outcast by his father, the Fire lord, but he continues his ongoing quest for the Avatar.

Master Pakku, a Waterbending master of the Northern Water Tribe, has set out for the South Pole, along with other Waterbenders from the North. They hope to help rebuild the Southern Water Tribe.

Aang will now learn Waterbending from Katara, who is on her way to becoming a Waterbending master. As of now, Sokka, Katara, and Aang have set off on Appa to journey to the Earth Kingdom. There, Aang hopes to find an Earthbending master to teach him so he can fulfill his destiny as the Avatar.

Now you know all that I know. Please, show this scroll only to those whom you would trust with your life. I must ask you to keep these sacred scrolls safe and hidden from prying eyes. The knowledge you have gained is a powerful tool, and the fate of four nations now rests in your hands. . . .